This
Judy Moody
Mood Journal
is the property of:

_____

- paste your picture here -

I started writing in my journal on _____.

My favorite page is _____.

If you read my journal, you'll put me in a _____ mood!

Revised edition 2009

ISBN 978-0-7636-2236-7 (first edition)
ISBN 978-0-7636-2736-2 (revised edition)

4 6 8 10 9 7 5 3

Printed in the United States of America

This book was typeset in Stone Informal and Judy Moody.
The illustrations were done in watercolor, tea, and ink.

Candlewick Press
99 Dover Street
Somerville, Massachusetts 02144

visit us at www.candlewick.com

Meet Judy Moody,
star of a hilarious series of
award-winning books by
Megan McDonald!

Judy Moody is independent-minded, an avid collector, a future doctor, and famous for her many moods: good moods, bad moods, and mad-face moods; goofy moods, grumpy moods, and glad moods.

This Judy Moody journal is perfect for writing about what puts *you* in a mood! It's also perfect for jotting down your favorite knock-knock jokes, making a Me collage, listing your favorite things, writing down your dreams, and lots more. So crack it open, sharpen your Grouchy pencil, and get started!

Judy was in a
positively purple,
on-top-of-spaghetti-and-the-world mood.

What Mood Are You In . . .

first thing in the morning?

_____

_____

_____

_____

_____

_____

on the first day of school?

_____

_____

_____

_____

_____

_____

when your brother or sister plays a trick on you?

_____

_____

_____

_____

_____

_____

_____

on your birthday?

_____

_____

_____

_____

_____

_____

_____

_____

_____

_____

_____

_____

_____

_____

_____

_____

_____

_____

Judy was in a mood. Not a good mood.
A bad mood. A mad-face mood.

Stink Stinks

Stink

- Judy's younger brother (aka "bother")
- Loves his pet, Toady
- Star of the Moody Hall of Fame

Do you have a nickname like Stink does?

_____

If you do, what is it?

_____

How do you think Stink got his nickname?

_____

_____

"Judy Moody" rhymes. Can you make your name rhyme?

_____

_____

_____

If anybody could put Judy in a bad mood, Stink could.
The baddest.

"Bothers" & Sisters

Do you have any brothers or sisters? What are their names and ages?

_____

_____

Do they ever bug you? How?

_____

_____

What's the funniest-trick-ever you played on your brother or sister?

_____

_____

_____

_____

GROUCHY
pencils—for
completely
impossible
moods.

HELP!
Even My Pencil's
in a Mood!

Design your own Grouchy pencil here:

If Stink were a volcano,
he would have spewed lava.

_____

_____

_____

_____

_____

_____

_____

_____

_____

_____

_____

_____

"Green means green with envy.
Green means you wish you were me."
—Judy Moody

Pizza, Zip, Zap . . .

Are you in a Spelling mood?

How many new words can you make from

Gino's Extra-Cheese Pizza?

List them here:

_____

_____

_____

_____

_____

_____

_____

_____

Ever since they had danced
the Maypole together in
kindergarten, Frank would
not leave Judy alone.

Best-Ever Stuff in the World

pizza table

lucky stone

5 pink pebbles

bubblegum fortune

blue lego

What's your favorite...

Color:
(Red, vermilion, pond-scum green?)

_____

_____

Game:
(Operation? Concentration?)

_____

_____

Book:
(Judy Moody Goes to Antarctica?
The "S" encyclopedia?)

_____

_____

Food:
(Jell-O? Pop Rocks?
Screamin' Mimi's ice cream?)

_____

_____

Movie:
(Godzilla Meets Jaws?)

_____

_____

Thing to collect:
(Pizza tables? Scabs?
Barbie doll heads?)

_____

_____

Judy licked her Rain Forest Mist scoop on top of Chocolate Mud, her favorite. She was in her best Judy Moody mood ever.

Funniest Thing Ever

Tell about the funniest thing that ever happened to you.

_____

_____

_____

_____

_____

_____

Worst Thing Ever

Tell about the worst thing that ever happened to you.

_____

_____

_____

CAVITY

_____

_____

_____

Yuckiest Thing Ever

Tell about the yuckiest thing that ever happened to you.

_____

_____

_____

_____

_____

She, Judy Moody, was definitely the one and only girl. . . . Frank Pearl's all-boy party had to be THE WORST THING THAT EVER HAPPENED to her.

Favorite Pets

Mouse

- Judy's cat
- Fond of bananas
- Makes toast

Toady

- Stink's toad
- Toad Pee Club mascot
- Was lost and found!

Do you have any pets?

_____

What are their names?

_____

_____

Write about a funny trick your pet can do.

_____

_____

_____

_____

_____

_____

If you could have any pet you wished for, what would it be?

_____

_____

_____

What would you name your new pet?

_____

_____

_____

Judy scooped up her cat and kissed him on the nose: "*Mww, mww, mww.* You are the best, most wonderful cat in the whole wide world with tuna fish on top."

Make a ME Collage!

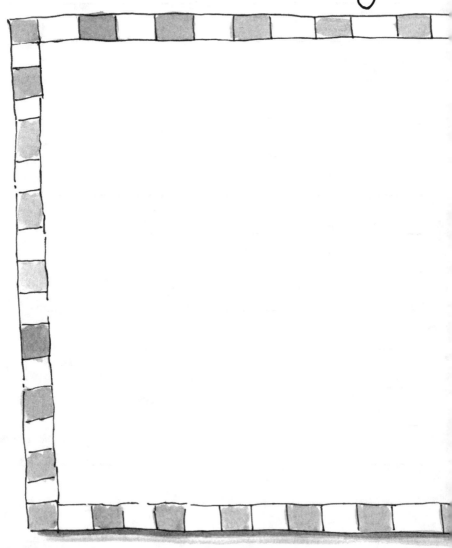

A ME Collage is a collage all about YOU!
Paste stuff (like pictures from magazines, photos, ticket stubs) here:
(BLUCK! No eating the paste!)

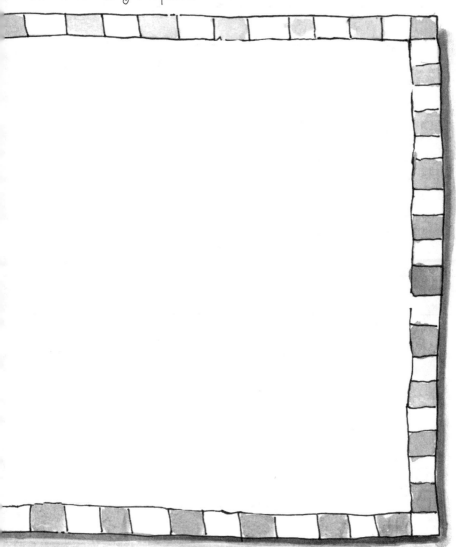

Judy tried to look like a person who would grow up to be a doctor and make the world a better place. A person who could turn a bad mood right around.

THE Toad Pee Club

Are you in a club?

_____

The name of Judy's club is the Toad Pee Club. What's the name of your club?

_____

_____

_____

_____

There was something warm and wet on his hand. Judy Moody and Rocky fell down laughing.

"Am I in the club yet?" asked Stink.

"Yes! Yes! Yes!" said Judy and Rocky.

"The Toad Pee Club!"

"Yippee!" cried Stink.

Emergency Meeting of the Toad Re Club today! Pass this to Rocky —J.M.

What do you do in your club?

_____

_____

_____

_____

_____

Write about a club you'd like to be in.

_____

_____

_____

_____

_____

_____

_____

Judy grabbed Mouse. "Mouse could be our new mascot!"

"The Mouse Pee Club? I don't think so," said Stink.

"See? If it wasn't for Toady, there wouldn't even be a Toad Pee Club."

Knock-Knocks

Write your own Knock-Knock Joke

Knock, Knock.

Who's there?

_____.

_____ who?

_____!

"Go away," said Judy.
"Knock, knock!" said Stink.
"Who's there?" said Judy.
"I, Stink," said Stink.
"I Stink who?"
"I stink you should let me
   in your room," said Stink,
   letting himself in anyway.

"Okay. Okay. I cannot
tell a lie. I coughed a
cherry pit at Stink."

Red in the Face

What makes you turn fire-engine red?

_____

_____

_____

_____

_____

Tell about your most embarrassing moment.

_____

_____

_____

_____

_____

All eyes were on Judy. She turned fire-engine red.
Hide-your-face-in-your-hands red. Big-fat-dictionary red.

Save the World!

How would YOU save the world?

_____

_____

_____

_____

_____

_____

_____

_____

One person! If all it took was one person,
then she, Judy Moody, could save the world!

In a
World-Saving
Mood

Saving the world was not going so well. . . .
So far, Judy had only saved four banana
peels, a lunch bag, and a toad.

Judy Moody

is

Batty for Band-Aids!

Design your own Band-Aid:

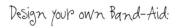

HEAL the WORLD

Dear Mr. Moody,
Congratulations! You are a winner in the Crazy Strips Design Your OWN Bandage Contest! Your design, Batty for Band-Aids, will be a featured Crazy Strip of the Month for October.
M. L. Donovan
CRAZY STRIPS C.E.O.

Stink had his own Crazy Strip! Her very own batty little brother was now as famous as Josephine Dickson, Inventor of the Adhesive Bandage.

My Room

Judy Moody's room has:
- A jelly bean collection
- Bunk beds
- Sock Monkey
- Doctor Kit
- Protect the Planet poster
- Mouse

My room has:

_____

_____

_____

My dream room has:

_____

_____

_____

Draw a picture of your dream room:

Best Friends

Judy Moody's Best Friends

Rocky

Frank

- Likes magic tricks
- Owns rubber hand
- Makes Judy laugh

- Eats paste
- Collects stuff
- Always there when you need him

Pick a friend. Make a list of stuff you like about him or her:

- _____

- _____

- _____

- _____

- _____

- _____

Draw a picture of your friend:

(name)

What really bugs you about your friend?

_____

_____

_____

_____

_____

_____

Write about a funny thing you did with your friend.

_____

_____

_____

_____

_____

_____

_____

_____

_____

_____

_____

_____

_____

_____

_____

_____

_____

"Same-same!" said Judy and Rocky, slapping hands together twice in a high-five, the way they always had when they did something exactly alike.

Judy could not help thinking how stupendous it would feel to be able to spell better than *meatloaf* and be the Queen Bee and wear a tiara.

Tiger-Striped Pajamas!

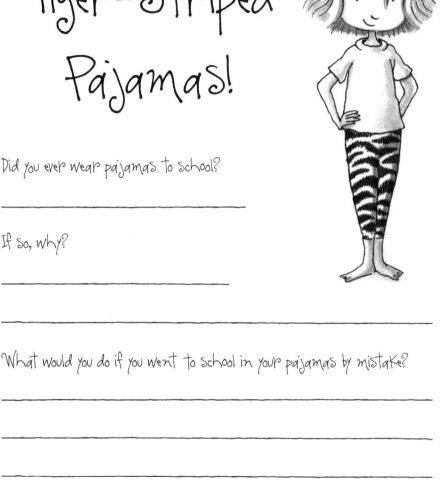

Did you ever wear pajamas to school?

_____

If so, why?

_____

_____

What would you do if you went to school in your pajamas by mistake?

_____

_____

_____

_____

_____

Moody Hall of Fame

Stink made his own Hall of Fame on the refrigerator.

In the Hall of Fame was:

- his report card
- a self-portrait that made him look like a monkey
- a photo of himself in his flag costume from the time he went to Washington, D.C., without Judy

If you could hang things on your refrigerator Hall of Fame, what would they be?

- _____
- _____
- _____
- _____

Famous!

Think of ways you might get your picture in the paper:

_____

_____

_____

_____

Write about getting your picture in the paper:

_____

_____

Draw a picture of yourself in the newspaper:

For
the first
time in
a long
time, the
once Judy
Muddy
felt more
famous
than an
elbow.

The Future You!

Predict your own future!
What would you like to be when you grow up?

_____

_____

_____

_____

_____

Where would you like to live?

_____

_____

_____

_____

_____

Is there anyone you admire? Would you like to be like them?
Why or why not?

_____

_____

_____

_____

_____

_____

_____

_____

_____

_____

_____

_____

_____

The future was
out there, waiting.
And there was
one more thing
Judy knew for
sure and absolute
positive—there
would be many
more moods to
come.

Which Judy Moody books have you read?

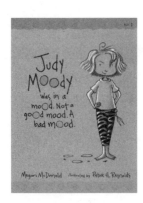

Judy Moody was in a mood. Not a good mood. A bad mood.

Megan McDonald Illustrated by Peter H. Reynolds

Judy Moody Predicts the Future

Megan McDonald Illustrated by Peter H. Reynolds

Judy Moody Around the World in 8½ Days

Megan McDonald Illustrated by Peter H. Reynolds

Be sure to check out Stink's adventures, too!

☐ Stink: The Incredible Shrinking Kid

☐ Stink and the Incredible Super-Galactic Jawbreaker

☐ Stink and the World's Worst Super-Stinky Sneakers

☐ Stink and the Great Guinea Pig Express

Judy Moody has her own website!

Visit **www.judymoody.com**
for all things Judy Moody and lots
of way-not-boring stuff to do, including:

- ☺ All you need to know about the best-ever
  Judy Moody Fan Club

- ☺ Answers to all your V.I.Q.s (very important
  questions) about Judy

- ☺ Way-not-boring stuff about Megan McDonald
  and Peter H. Reynolds

- ☺ Double-cool activities that will be sure to put you
  in a mood—and not a bad mood, a good mood!

- ☺ Totally awesome T.P. Club info!

DOUBLE RARE!